and cast it
from you

SCARLETT R. ALGEE

COLD WAR
RADIO
PRESS

This is a work of fiction. All of the characters, names, incidents, organizations, and dialogue in this novel are either the products of the author's imagination or are used fictitiously.

"And Cast It From You" was originally published in September 2020 as episode TWL 1013 of the *Wicked Library* podcast.

ISBN: 978-1-7343897-5-3 (chapbook)

First printing edition: November 4, 2024
Printed by Cold War Radio Press in the United States of America.
Cover Design: Don Noble | Cover Layout: Scarlett R. Algee

Cold War Radio Press
201 Lake Street
Ridgely, TN 38080

Many thanks to Nelson, Nora, and William

and cast it from you

IT STARTS ON A Tuesday afternoon.

I can say with certainty, at least, that the house is fine. When my grandmother went into hospice care a few weeks before she passed, I had the house professionally cleaned. If I were feeling generous, I could say I wanted it to look nice for all the visitors who'd crowd in after the funeral. But since I'm feeling honest, I only did it because I knew I'd be moving in and wanted to spare myself some work.

That sounds selfish, and I don't mean for it to. Grammy and I had always been close, even when I went halfway across the country to go to college, even when I landed the job I'd always wanted, a hundred miles from home. As a kid I'd climbed all the trees and worn out multiple tire swings and eaten enough apple pie to fill an Olympic-sized swimming pool. After my mom died, Grammy had said I'd always have a home with her if I wanted it. Sure, this move was going to balloon my ten-minute daily commute to a ninety-minute drive each way, but I'd been more than thrilled at the idea of getting out of my tiny one-bedroom apartment and never paying rent or listening to the other tenants' screaming kids again.

But. Tuesday.

The shed is not fine. I'd found the key, still pristine, in the kitchen's junk drawer, but the padlock it had fit into was so rusted it had practically broken off in my hand. My guess is that Grammy had locked it tight after my grandfather died twenty years earlier, and had never ventured in there since.

I lean on my broom and drag a plastic-gloved hand across my forehead, smearing grime, and decide that I couldn't have been more right.

This place is a wreck. One corner is just a stack of empty red plastic gasoline cans, caked inside with brown residue and brittle with age, towering almost to the ceiling. Another holds the bicycle I'd learned to ride when I was eight, now rusting away under a moldy, water-stained sheet. Grammy's old Singer sewing machine and its table take up part of the wall under the lone window, surrounded by boxes of piled fabric scraps that look to have provided bedding for generations of mice.

And the dust. Sweet Jesus Christ, the *dust*.

It's pale yellow, like sand, and fine as powdered sugar, and at least two inches thick on every horizontal surface—more like four in the corners. It coats my tongue with every breath and tastes like sawdust, and I know that because as soon as I'd taken two steps in here, I'd sucked a mouthful of it in and sneezed it back out, sending pillowy little clouds of it swirling—right in my face, in my hair, between my teeth.

I'd run back into the house for a mask after that, cursing myself for not thinking of one in the first place, for thinking the worst threat would be loose planks or water damage or a lone rusty bicycle. Still, even with a mask on now, I've sneezed ten times in twenty minutes. My throat is gritty and my eyes are starting to burn. I can't believe I'd thought a broom and a pair of gloves would be sufficient. I'd had plans to make this into a little creative space, a sewing room or studio; I never expected this. First mistake.

Scratch that. My first mistake had been not having this place cleaned along with the house, or better yet, razed to the ground, though that gives me the mental image of the collapsing shed billowing out a mushroom cloud of faintly wood-flavored nastiness that would blanket the house or even the town.

I can't even laugh at that. The mask won't fit my face properly, and even swearing to myself is just a guaranteed way to get another mouthful of particulate filth. Even after I remembered Grammy's old trick of wrapping the head of the broom in a damp towel before slowly, assiduously attacking the mess in the corners, there's more dust swirling in the air, sticking to my skin and the folds of my clothes, glittering in the odd ray of sunlight, than in the carefully-collected knee-high pile I've amassed in the middle of the floor. Every stroke of the broom leaves a trail behind, a silver streak of decay.

I sneeze again, again, a third time. Tears burst from my eyes and run down inside my mask, the wet streaks on my face acting as instant dust magnets. Coughing through tightly clamped teeth, I prop the broom against the wall and head for the door.

This is going to take another professional.

***

Back in the house, I strip out of my mask and gloves and filthy clothes in the mud room and head straight for the bathroom. When I move, I feel grit in the sweaty creases of my elbows and knees; there's even dust between my toes, which means sweeping again to get up the traces I'm leaving behind.

I'd prefer a bath in the tub, but the idea of sitting in a floating layer of filth turns my stomach, so shower it is. Under the hottest water I can stand, I scrub myself three times and wash my hair twice. I turn the cold tap to lower the temperature and shove my face under the spray, letting water fill my nostrils and huffing it out, opening my mouth so I can gargle and swish and spit. Over and over, I collect tepid water in my pruning fingers and scour my eyes. Afterward, I dry off thoroughly, pull on the t-shirt and shorts I'd hung from the towel rack, shove my other clothes into a trash bag to deal with later, and take to the floors of the hallway and kitchen with a wet mop.

By the time the dust is dealt with, my muscles are starting to shiver and ache from exertion. Still, I don't quite feel clean, so I wash my hands and feet and face again. I brush my teeth twice and gulp down two Advil PM tablets with a glass of cold tea. Maybe there was some pollen mixed in that grime; I've already got a little tickle in my throat, a sniffle starting, and a vague itch under my eyelids. Hell, maybe it's mold.

I put in a call to the same people who'd cleaned up the house, and get an appointment for Thursday. Not as soon as I'd like, but better than putting myself through that again.

Then I grab my tea and my phone and go lie down across the end of the bed, ready to play Words with Friends until the antihistamine kicks in. I'm still on bereavement leave, after all; I don't have to go anywhere.

***

When I wake up, the bedroom's dark and I'm disoriented. The irritation in my throat is gone except for a little drainage, but my mouth's so dry my tongue has glued itself to my teeth, and it feels furry when I pry it loose. Getting my eyes open takes a few stinging blinks; they're gummy, the lashes wet with something thick. I fumble for my phone and wake it up to check the time, and my optic nerves shriek at the brightness of the screen. Wednesday, just after one AM. I feel like I've slept all night.

I use the phone's light to find my tea glass, but it's empty. I need water, and to see what's going on with my eyes.

Getting out of bed takes effort. My thighs and shoulders aren't happy with all the cleaning I tried to do earlier, and my spine pops in multiple places when I finally sit up. One painful step at a time, I make it into the bathroom. For a few moments, when I turn on the light, I'm agonizingly blind. Then my pupils adjust, and I stare at myself. The edges of my nostrils are red, the corners of my lips cracked. Above them, the whites of my eyes aren't't white but pink; there's an odd prickling sensation in the right one, and a thin angry red line along the bottom of my right iris.

I must've blown a blood vessel, doing all that sneezing. My eyes are itchy, the lids thick with clear gunk, but I resist the urge to scrub them with my fists like a child. Instead I turn the cold water on and wipe my eyelids off carefully with my fingertips. The cold is soothing, so I do a second rinse, and remember the fresh bottle of Visine in the medicine cabinet.

Already they're less red, but I'm sore all over and still groggy from that Advil. I pad into the kitchen and drink two glasses of water from the tap, then fetch a cold bottle of tea from the fridge. Yawning, and feeling my jaw pop as I do, I make my way back to bed.

No more housework for me. I had awful allergies as a kid, and the last thing I want is for that to crop back up. So I drink my tea and lie in bed and think of things I need to do to the house: paint the shutters, ditch Grammy's beloved old rotary phone—maybe I can sell it on eBay as a novelty—and get one of those smart doorbells installed. I haven't been here in over a decade, after all, and I've already heard more than one neighbor grumble about porch pirates and mangled packages.

And the shed, of course. I need to do something about the shed.

***

When I wake up the second time, I immediately know something is wrong.

Liquid leaks from my right eye as soon as I open it. I smear it away with my knuckles, but my vision's too blurry to make anything out on that side, so I squeeze the sore lids shut and focus with my left. The goo is thin like pus, and light yellow, like that dust I'd been trying to sweep up in the shed. Is that's what's leaking out? Did I get that much of the stuff in my system?

I stumble back into the bathroom and rinse everything away again, but this time it doesn't feel better: the cold water on the surface of my eye burns like acid, and the weird prickly sensation has gotten stronger. And the irritation—

My left eye is better, clearer. The bottom half of the right one is now flaming red like it's full of blood, the lids livid and swollen. A trickle of yellow liquid streams out as I watch. I try the Visine again, but the redness remover seems to bite into the sensitive tissue, and I grab onto the sink as scalding tears, both clear and yellowish, pour down my face. I'm panting like a dog, trying to keep my suddenly roiling stomach at bay.

When the discomfort passes a little I try to pull my aching eyelids up, to see if they're red underneath, but even touching them produces another wave of nausea. I breathe through my teeth and do another cold rinse, and go in search of my phone.

There's only one ophthalmologist nearby, a Dr. Simmons in the next town. The receptionist is sympathetic, if entirely too perky for early morning. The doctor can see me Thursday morning, she chirps: exactly the same time as the shed-cleaning I'd scheduled, though I guess I don't need to actually be here for that.

It sounds like pink eye, she tells me, though we need to be sure it's not a bacterial infection. Use cold compresses and take Benadryl and try not to touch it.

Almost immediately, my eye starts itching like mad.

***

"That is one impressive case of conjunctivitis," Dr. Simmons says.

I'm a little surprised that the eye doctor's a woman, though I can't say why; maybe because the town feels so small right now. I'm more surprised that I actually managed to drive here, with my vision half obscured by the gunk oozing from my sore eye. The receptionist had actually squeaked in shock when I'd walked in and given her my name.

I just nod, moving my head as little as possible. Her ophthalmoscope's light had been too bright and too warm, sending a lance of agony through my brain and leaving wavering ghostly afterimages of my own retinas dancing in my vision. "So how do we treat this? And why isn't it in both eyes?"

She shrugs. "You said you were wearing a mask while you were trying to clean up the shed, but no safety goggles. Did you rub your eyes?"

Safety goggles. I hadn't even thought of them. And I want to say that no, I hadn't rubbed my eyes, I'd been too busy sneezing and anyway I'd had gloves on...but. "I don't know," I admit. "I just don't know. I could have, I guess? That dust was pretty thick, and it seemed to get everywhere."

"Then you could have a corneal abrasion," the doctor says, "and that would increase the risk of inflammation like this. Tell you what. I want you to get some baby shampoo and wash your eyelids three times a day—and be careful at it, that's probably still gonna burn pretty badly if it gets in—and I'll give you some steroid drops and an antibiotic ointment. And a work note—I'm pretty sure this is allergic, but better to err on the side of caution for a few days."

"I'm not working right now," I say. "My grandmother died ten days ago and I'm still on bereavement leave until Monday...although my boss *does* want me to come in tomorrow so she can catch me up before I start back."

"Hmm. Well, try not to touch your face or shake hands with anybody, and I'd like to see you back next week." Dr. Simmons doesn't sound pleased, but at least her first words weren't the *I'm so sorry* that I'm already tired of hearing. She goes to the exam room door and flips the overhead lights back on, and watches me wince. "You're awfully light sensitive. Let's add a patch while we're at it."

***

I'm in the pharmacy line with my eye patch and my prescriptions when my phone buzzes. Ordinarily I'd ignore it, but there are six people ahead of me, and the onscreen number belongs to that cleaning company. "Hello?"

"Miss Winters?" It's the owner, a man named Harry or Henry or something like that. I hadn't really paid attention the first time; I'd just paid the bill. "I needed to talk to you about that shed."

"Oh, right. Hey, sorry, I had to get out to see a doctor, but the padlock on the door broke off, so you shouldn't have any trouble—"

"I got a man on-site," he interrupts. "Listen, we got a problem. Marty can't finish the job today, he says there's something in that building making him feel sick."

Don't I know it, I think, and manage to clumsily dab my eye with a wad of tissue. The sooner I can get this patch on, maybe the sooner people will stop staring like I've got an eyeball plague. "Yeah, sorry, it's been shut up for twenty years and it's really a mess, so if we need to reschedule—"

"Miss Winters, I think this is a little beyond our scope," Harry/Henry/whatever says. "You said yourself that there was water damage, which makes me think we're looking at a mold case."

I'd thought that in the midst of the filth. *Maybe it's mold.* "So what should I do?"

"I sent Marty home, and I'm on the way to see it for myself," he says. "But don't worry. If it needs a mold remediation specialist, I know some good ones."

"Thanks," I say, wondering if I'll get a bill for whatever's wrong with Marty. And when I get home an hour later, true to the man's word, there's a business card for mold remediation taped to the storm door.

On the back of it is scrawled, *Try to stay out of the shed.*

***

I tack the business card to the fridge with a magnet and promptly forget about it. Checking in with my boss tomorrow is too important, so I get to work with my pharmacy haul.

Washing my inflamed eyelids with baby shampoo feels like dragging coarse-grained sandpaper across them, or so I can easily imagine. At the same time, it brings back memories of my mom washing my hair when I was five. The scent of the stuff hasn't changed a bit. The other meds are harder: my right eye's lids really don't want to open fully, and really *are* impressively swollen—but I grit my teeth and force them apart with my fingers, wincing at the ripping pain. The ointment isn't bad—squeeze a thin grey line onto a freshly-washed finger and smear it in there, anticipating blurry vision and greasy tears—but the steroid drops are worst, bringing back the burn and bite as though the surface of my eye bears a thousand cuts.

I think about what Dr. Simmons had said about corneal abrasion, and I worry. Could I really have scratched my eye so badly? Did the grit and dust from the shed somehow get inside my eye? Is it in there now, slicing at my retina from the inside? Am I going to go blind?

In the bathroom medicine cabinet I find a mostly-full bottle of Valium and one of Lortabs, both predating Grammy's hospice stay but still recent enough to be safe.

I take one of each and go to bed with my tea.

***

I don't want to make too many repeat performances out of the benzo-and-painkiller combination, but at least it had numbed the pain in my eye enough for me to sleep last night. Getting the meds in this morning requires scrubbing caked-up crud off my eyelids first, and trying not to stare at the steadily-spreading redness washing over my eye, or at the torrent of pus that breaks loose once everything's fully open. I feel like my face will never be clean again.

The patch is going to be a problem. Maybe there's some expensive properly-fitted version I could have gotten with a prescription, but the one I'd grabbed off the shelf feels too big and too sharp around the sides, the inner edge of it pressing uncomfortably into the tender corner of my eye and the side of my nose. In the mirror I look like the worst-prepared pirate ever, so I pull it off to save for actually going inside at work.

I need ninety minutes to get to the office from the new house. That should feel exciting, *the new house*, but the only sensation the idea provokes is that of dust filming every surface. I keep touching my face despite the doctor's orders, rubbing my fingertips together, expecting to feel tiny shards of grit catching in the ridges of my fingertips.

I wolf down toast and tea and half an apple, and leave the house thirty minutes earlier than I need to. Which turns out to be a good thing: my vision keeps smearing and doubling, and four times I have to pull to the side of the highway and swipe a fresh layer of effluvium from my cheek. By the time I pull into my designated parking space, somehow ten minutes early despite all the stops, I've rubbed a raw spot into my face and stripped off half my makeup, and that prickle inside my eye is now a weird, sickening crawly feeling. I put the patch on gingerly, stuff some clean tissues into the pocket of my jacket, and feel thankful for once that I'd only had to use mascara on one side.

I walk in expecting my coworkers to ask questions or make jokes, but nothing like that happens. A couple of them express their condolences about Grammy and ask how I'm holding up, but for the most part they take in the patch and the redness of my cheek, and their gazes slide uncomfortably away. No one actually asks what's happened, though I wish they would; it would be easier to take than the glances and whispers.

My boss, Theresa, raises her eyebrows when she sees my face, but she doesn't say anything until I'm safely in her office and she's got my clients' accounts pulled up on her laptop. "So, two weeks back out in the old country home and you've already poked your eye out, Kris?"

There's a little fixedness in her gaze as she says it, a little desperation that I'll find the question funny, and I can't help it. I grin, even though I immediately wince as the expression tightens my eyelids. "Something like that. Doc says it's an abrasion. I went on a cleaning spree and ended up scratching my eyeball with my work gloves."

"That's definitely doing it wrong." Theresa grimaces in sympathy, but then she squares her shoulders and turns the laptop's screen toward me. "Okay, if you can see to take a few notes on your phone, let's go over what's changed while you've been out."

Forty-five minutes later, I have enough information stashed in OneNote that I can get back into the stream of things next week with ease. I'm also on my third tissue, having had to devote one hand to dabbing at the bottom of the patch to keep it from leaking. Theresa watches with her lips thinned and her nose wrinkled, and suddenly it dawns on me that the goo has developed a smell. Maybe it's from the ointment.

"Kris, are you sure you'll be ready to go on Monday?" Theresa asks as I stand to walk out. She starts to put a hand on my shoulder, but drops it as the idea of being touched anywhere near my face makes me flinch. "That eye seems pretty bad."

"Ah, I'm just having an allergic reaction to go with the scratch," I say. "It's only been twenty-four hours since I started the meds, I'm sure it'll be much better by then."

"If you say so," she answers dubiously, shifting in her seat. "You know what? Go ahead and take next week. Get that looked at again. It might be contagious and I really don't need half my staff coming down with...with *that*."

I'll be fine by Monday, I want to say, but I don't believe it either. On the way back to my car, I spend five minutes in the office bathroom, rinsing my eye out and washing down the patch with disinfectant soap.

The whispers and stares follow me out.

***

Halfway home, just as rain starts splattering the windshield, I get a call.

Hearing the ring through the car's speakers startles me. It's what's his name from the cleaning company again, and I grit my teeth and pull over for what is, by my own count, the ninth time. "Hello."

"Miss Winters?" Static makes his voice scratchy. "It's Henry. I just wanted to follow up and see if you'd called that mold specialist yet."

Oh. So that's his name. "No," I admit. "I had to drive into the office today, so I haven't had time, but I'm on my way home now, I'll do it when I get there." This must be about whatever happened to Marty. "I haven't been back in that shed, either. What's going on?"

"Eh, Marty's wife called, he's in the hospital," Henry says. "Looks like he's got a pretty serious fungal infection, so—"

"So what?" Yep, this is it; I'm getting a bill. "Look, I didn't ask for the damned shed to be so filthy, okay? And how is he sick already? He was in there, what, an hour, tops? I'm really sorry, but just send me a bill for his ER visit or whatever and—"

"He's been admitted." Henry's voice has gone soft. "Miss Winters, look, nobody's sending you a bill, okay? It's not your fault. I just want you to know what's going on so you can get it taken care of and maybe not get sick yourself."

Yeah, well, too late for that. Still, I huff my breath out and try to calm down. I'm still wearing the patch, I realize, and my face is wet; I pull the dripping thing off and drop it in the passenger floorboard. "Sorry. Sorry, I didn't mean to blow up at you, things are just"—I root for a fresh Kleenex—"difficult."

"Sure. Sure." He's meek now, apologetic. "I just wanted to let you know, so you won't go haring back in there. I think it's past saving, myself."

Like my eye? I want to ask, but I bite it back. This will get better, though I probably need to let Dr. Simmons know about the fungus. "Thank you. Really. I'll take it into consideration." I watch the rain run down the glass and flick my wipers on. "Right now I have to get back on the road."

Back home, in the rain, I use a rubber glove to pick up the filthy eye patch, and scrub the hell out of the floorboard.

***

Saturday is a blur. Ointment. Drops. Benadryl. Two hours of unpacking books and knickknacks, of stabbing pain through my eye socket every time I bend to reach into a box. Ointment. Drops. Baby shampoo. Tea. Ointment. Drops. Valium. Lortab. Four-hour nap. Half an hour of Netflix that's too blurry to follow properly. Three minutes of a Sudoku app on my phone, before the screen is too bright to continue. Ointment. Drops. Benadryl, water, more tea. The smell of the discharge is definitely worse, like the sweet rot of an overripe tomato. No wonder Theresa had had that look on her face.

I'm hydrating too much, and the gunk's not drying up. Or I'm not hydrating enough, and that's making the inflammation worse. The meds just need more time. The meds aren't strong enough. The lids of my right eye are the color of an unhealed bruise, and when it's not time to put in the ointment or the drops, I give up on trying to keep them open. The patch is deep in the trash, inside a few layers of newspaper.

Nothing can hold my attention against the constant itch and burn. I keep shoving my knuckles into my eye socket for a few seconds of relief that blossoms right back into agony, into that crawling prickling hell, and so I keep rushing to wash my hands and reapply drops. Soon my knuckles are as raw as my tear-glazed face, and I'm wishing I had vodka in the house, because a shot glass to the eyeball has begun to sound like it can't possibly hurt worse.

Dr. Simmons isn't in the office on Saturdays, but I call and leave a message anyway, telling her I'll be in on Monday. Telling, not asking for an appointment. I'm past appointments. Something has to be done, and soon.

I double up on the painkillers and fall across the bed, whimpering like a baby, feeling liquid ooze out onto the pillowcase.

***

I wake up again, and for the first time in days, my eye is dry.

I reach out for my phone to check the time, but it's not on the mattress next to me. I feel around, and realize I'm not on the mattress either.

The bedroom is carpeted, but I'm on a hardwood floor. Something is stuck to my face, to my lips, in my throat.

No. Oh God. Oh *no*. I push myself upright with my hands, and for a few seconds there's enough adrenaline in my system to shut out the pain and bring both eyes wide open.

I'm in the shed, and I'm covered in dust.

I scramble to my feet, grabbing onto the old sewing machine for support as the world swims around me. I sneeze and cough and cough again, hard, retching, trickling bile down the front of my t-shirt. My inflamed eye is a churning cauldron of agony, of internal pinpricks like the scuttling of sharp-tipped limbs.

How the hell did I get in here? *When* the hell did I get in here?

I cough and sneeze and retch again, drag a palm over my face and pull away a handful of yellow powder. It's in my teeth and on my tongue and caked to the lashes of my right eye, and as I spit and snivel and vomit for real this time, liquid bursts out of my livid eyelids, thicker and hotter than before.

The door is gaping open. I bolt for the house, my bare feet sliding on the wet grass. This time I don't even bother shucking my clothes at the door; I just make a mad dash for the bathroom, catching myself on the sink so I don't land on my ass, the jarring stop sending a fresh gush from my eye.

I look in the mirror and scream.

It isn't pus or tears.

It's blood.

***

I sit on the narrow bed in the equally narrow ER cubicle, elbows over my bent head to try to shield myself from the stabbing white light, and sob openly, watching my eyes drip onto the papery gown barely covering my dignity. Clear from one. Yellow from the other, and red, so much red.

I don't completely remember getting here. Stripping down to get under the shower and get the filth off me, yes; running the spray hot and turning my face into it and just screaming and screaming, and getting out with this wrecked eye still leaking blood. Getting dressed and getting in the car are a complete blank, though apparently I'd had the presence of mind to bring the drops and ointment along.

Someone knocks on the door, and I force myself to look up. It's not the nurse who'd nervously taken my vitals earlier; it's a guy with a stethoscope slung around his neck. That's about as much as I can make out with my increasingly unreliable vision: his name tag is just a blur against his green scrubs. He sanitizes his hands and snaps on gloves and comes up to read my wristband.

"So, Kris Winters, right? Hold your head up for me," he says brightly, already taking a penlight from a pocket. "And I'm sorry, but this is going to hurt."

Of course it is. I grit my teeth down hard and manage not to yell when he pulls my eyelids open, but a whine slips out anyway, and the little beam is breathtakingly hot. Then he turns off the penlight and pulls away from my face, and I bury my face protectively in my hands.

The doctor pulls up a stool to the edge of the bed. "Okay, yeah," he says. "We're looking at severe conjunctivitis here. And I know what you said about the dust and the coughing and sneezing"—he flips through the thin paper chart that's been thrown together for me—"but your airways sound good, so I don't see this being an allergy problem. Most likely you've scratched your eye and some bacteria got in."

I think of Marty and wonder if he's in this hospital right now. "Not a fungus?"

The doctor makes a thoughtful face and shakes his head. "This fast? Not really seeing it. Still, I guess it needs to be ruled out." He sucks his teeth. "You said you were seeing Dr. Simmons tomorrow, and you can do that if you want, but I'd rather send you home with a couple of days of oral antibiotics and set you up with somebody who's got a bit more training. Obviously your current regimen isn't doing the job." He flips the chart closed and sits back. "Your call."

The idea of having to do more driving to give another stranger yet *another* description makes my head hurt right now. "Just give me the pills and I'll take my chances."

***

"It's just not letting up, is it?" Dr. Simmons glances through the chart copy she'd had faxed from the hospital. "I think 'severe' is an understatement at this point, but I'm not sure I'd be so quick to call it a fungal infection either. It's been less than a week."

I tell her about Marty and what his boss had said. I don't tell her about my—my *sleep-wallowing* face-down in the muck on the shed floor. I've never sleepwalked before, and my gut says it's unwise to let her know I've been mixing pills. "Do you think the guy from the ER was right? I need some kind of...extra-specialist to look at this?"

"Maybe." She lays the chart aside and picks up her ophthalmoscope, flicking the overhead lights off. "I'm really sorry to keep putting you through this."

"It's just your job." I accept the nitrile gloves she offers me, pull them on and cover my left eye with my palm protectively, as if I can save it from whatever's happening to its twin. Pink eye spreads, right?

Then I grit my teeth hard, grasp my afflicted eyelids with the first two fingers of my right hand, and *yank*.

I don't recognize my own voice in the wounded-animal noise that comes out of my mouth. All I recognize is the explosion of pain twisting through my eye and burrowing into the socket, the splatter of hot fluid down my face, the whiff of decay. Dr. Simmons inhales sharply and turns away from me in a hurry; she roots through a drawer, and when she turns back to me, she's put on a pair of yellow paper surgical masks.

She smiles, or I think she does. It's hard to tell, but the corners of her eyes have crinkled. "You really don't need me breathing on that," she says, and lifts the scope. "Okay. Try to hold still."

Then there's light in my eye, brilliant and blazing, like I'm suddenly looking through the facets of a diamond. My eye leaks more and I bite the inside of my cheek, fighting the urge to cry out and look away. I get that wraithlike glimpse of my retinal pattern again: is it me, or is that a blotch?

"Kris. Kris, hold still, you're squirming." The doctor's voice has gone stern, and it snaps my attention back to her. "Stop. There's something in here and I can't see."

There's something in here. That's enough to make me rigid in my hard plastic seat, to make me scissor my shrieking eyelids further open. More light gets in and for a second I feel a distinct scratching inside my head, as though something with a lot of legs is flexing them, testing them out.

I squeak, but Dr. Simmons misinterprets my distress. "It's okay," she murmurs, "it's okay...wow, it's really red back there, it looks like—*ohJesusChrist.*"

She straightens up for a second, open-mouthed. She's seen it, I think. She's seen whatever the hell just moved inside my eye. But she leans in with the scope again, and the boiling sensation of the light leaves anything I could have asked shriveled and hanging on my tongue.

"That...is...not good." Off goes the scope; Dr. Simmons lays it down and pulls the masks off, taking a seat next to the counter. "Nothing wrong with your vitals? No recent head trauma while you've been working in the house?"

Head trauma? Was that what happened in the shed yesterday? Did I crawl around in there and lie down, or did I pass out and hit something after all those pills? Wouldn't I be banged up? "No," I answer, and realize I'm still holding my eye open. I let go and moan in relief as a wad of tissues is crammed into my hand. "What's going on?"

"You," Dr. Simmons answers grimly, "have had one heck of a retinal hemorrhage. The back of your eye looks like half-chewed cherry Jello." She drums her fingers absently on my chart folder. "You're not diabetic and you're not hypertensive. So yes, I have a colleague you really need to see." She gets up. "Let me make a phone call right now. Don't move."

I want to move. I want to get up and run, or at least shove this blood-soaked ball of Kleenex into my eye socket and grind until whatever's in there stops *itching*.

Instead, I sit still.

***

Another business card, this time for a Dr. Ripley. Retinal specialist. First thing tomorrow. Maybe my retina's about to detach; maybe I'll need surgery. The very thought makes my gut roil and makes the crawly sensation in my eye flex and stretch.

Another pharmacy run: a second patch, because the look of sickened disbelief from the pharmacist makes me regret trashing the first one, and lidocaine drops. Dr. Simmons' voice had stayed steely as she wrote out the script, never regaining its softer patter: *Ordinarily we use these for things like cataract surgeries, but you definitely need some relief. Use them when you get home—let's say every four hours, in your case. And if they don't help, tell Dr. Ripley first thing tomorrow. He'll have other options.*

On the way out, I visit the pharmacy's restroom, crank up the hot water, and load up on soap. Then I wash my face and my hands and my eyelashes. Maybe it's not the best and safest cleanup job, but I want to try those lidocaine drops as soon as I get to the car.

It's awkward in the confines of the driver's seat, and I howl when I have to force my eyelids open again. The liquid is thicker than I expected, almost like a gel, and a little difficult to squeeze out of the bottle. But two drops splat onto the surface of my eye, and immediately it feels like I've squirted lighter fluid in there and tossed in a match. My instinct is to grab a tissue and scrub the stuff out right away, but I just take hold of the steering wheel and breathe through my mouth and wait, and slowly, slowly, the pain settles down. The crawly feeling in my eye subsides, as though something's turned over and gone to sleep. The burning itch dies down—still niggling but lessened, something I can almost ignore.

"Goddamn," I say aloud in surprise. "It's a miracle."

***

The shed door's still open when I get home. I'd forgotten to close it after the incident yesterday.

I don't want to go near it, but I don't want to risk anyone getting in and seeing those gas cans and having ideas, either. The turmoil in my eye has settled down and a headache has begun to stir in its place, a low pulse lancing through my head at each step.

It's not till I'm at the shed that I remember the broken padlock; I've got no way to secure the door. But just inside, I glimpse a concrete block I'd skirted around when I'd started cleaning; it should at least hold things shut until I can get my poor eye in better shape.

I take a deep breath of fresh, damp outside air and step over the threshold to grab the block. It's heavier than expected and drags at my grip, making my fingertips sting, and when I crouch to get a better hold, everything wheels and blurs—

—and when my senses clear I'm on my knees, the block forgotten as I lift a scoop of sandy dust halfway to my mouth, a skittering sensation now alive inside my eye as if something's wriggling, excited—

What the fuck am I *doing*? What is *wrong* with me?

I shake off that handful of dust and gag, stumbling back outside, grabbing onto the door to keep myself on my feet.

I run for the house and don't look back.

***

By the time I get inside, my heart's pounding, and the lidocaine is wearing off. By the time the appointment card for the retinal specialist has gone on the fridge, beside the one for the mold remediation service I still haven't called, I'm shaking all over as agony thrashes through my skull.

I need more drops. More pills. More *something*.

I scrabble in the medicine cabinet, scattering bottles into the sink. The tube of antibiotic ointment clatters against the porcelain and I snatch it up, squeeze out a thick line, jam it into my eye. It burns like hellfire and my head throbs, and inside my eye there's a sick *twisting* sensation.

Then something jabs outward through my sclera, and my already blurry vision goes dark.

For a long moment I'm paralyzed, panting, drooling helplessly onto the items in the sink. Touching the surface of my right eye brings a wash of weakness and the feel of something stiff beneath my fingers, making me drag my heavy gaze to the mirror.

My left eye's blurry until I blink a few times; then it focuses, and there they are, two slender deep-red stems sticking out of my right eye like prongs.

And then one of them moves.

I scream and scramble backward, my ass hitting the edge of the bathtub. Something's in my eye. Something's *alive* inside my eye.

I know what I have to do, and it can't wait for tomorrow.

***

I shake pills out into my hand—Valium, Lortab, Benadryl—without counting, and chew, and guzzle water from the tap. I grope blurrily into the kitchen and pull a grapefruit spoon from the silverware drawer. I snap the tip from the bottle of lidocaine drops and tilt my head back and pour. I go back into the bathroom and sit on the floor at the side of the tub, and lay my phone down within easy reach. I pour in the rest of the drops. I'm running on adrenaline, but for how long?

The drugs kick in fast and hard—I'm dizzy, queasy, drooling again—but I can feel the surface of my eye breaking, pinprick by pinprick.

It's time.

Everything's heavy now, slow. My head weighs a ton. My upper eyelid feels weird in my fingers: rubbery like silicone, like something detached from me. This time it stretches easily over the sharp tip and teeth of the spoon, the discomfort fuzzy and distant until somewhere, metal meets bone. Then it's torture again, limbs scraping, flailing for purchase inside my eye.

The jolt of agony clears my mind enough to let me tighten my grip on the spoon, to take one deep breath, before I swing my head forward and slam the end of the spoon into the bathtub's rim.

There's a ripping noise and a gush of hot liquid. In the darkness rearing to swallow me, someone screams, and I think it's me.

***

Slowly, so slowly, I wake up.

Raising my head sends a spike of fresh torment through my skull, though at least the rush of blood seems to be drying. I brace myself on the edge of the tub and paw at my phone, managing to hit the side buttons enough to fumble an emergency call through.

The edges of my vision—what's left of it—are growing black, but I squint and strain and manage to focus on what's in the tub: the spoon, black in a pool of jellied blood, and what's left of my right eye.

The dangling shred of optic nerve is purple and unraveled. The surface of the eye itself has split open, spilling tacky pink liquid and a small mountain of sand-colored dust, and beside it a dark red, spider-like creature rests on its back, dead legs curled inward.

My breath stirs the dust, and this time it doesn't drift; it rolls, rounded, like tiny eggs.

Nausea clenches at my gut and forces me to lie back. The 911 call has connected but I can't say anything, only pant and groan as a fresh wave of darkness washes over me.

And as my vision dims, softly, ever so insidiously, my left eye begins to itch.

about the author

SCARLETT R. ALGEE'S FICTION has been published by *Body Parts Magazine, Bards and Sages Quarterly*, and *The Wicked Library*, among other places. Her short story "Dark Music," written for the podcast *The Lift*, was a 2016 Parsec Awards finalist, and her flash-fiction piece "Bone Deep" was a 2020 Pushcart Prize nominee.

She published her debut collection, *Bleedthrough and Other Small Horrors* (Cold War Radio Press) in 2020, and skulks on X at @scarlettralgee and on Reddit as u/Cold_War_Radio, where she mostly lurks on game and crafting subs and argues about *Skyrim*.